## For Ella and Riley

Published by The Ella Riley Group, Unit 1b, Stean Street Studios, 3-5 Dunston Road, London E8 4EH

www.davinahamilton.com

© The Ella Riley Group 2017

All rights reserved. Without limiting the rights under copyright reserved above, no part of this publication may be reproduced, stored in or introduced into a retrieval system, or transmitted in any form or by any means (electronic, mechanical, photocopying, recording or otherwise), without the prior written permission of both the copyright owner and the above publisher of this book.

A catalogue record of this book is available from the British Library.

ISBN: 978-0-9957005-0-5

# RILEY CAN BE ANYTHING

Words by Davina Hamilton
Illustration by Elena Reinoso

Riley loved his big cousin Joe,
There were so many things Joe wanted to know.
Like "How does honey come from bees?"
And "Why must I always say 'thank you' and 'please'?"

Big cousin Joe was full of questions,
And big cousin Joe had lots of suggestions.
This time he asked Riley: "Can you tell me,
"When you grow up, what are you going to be?"

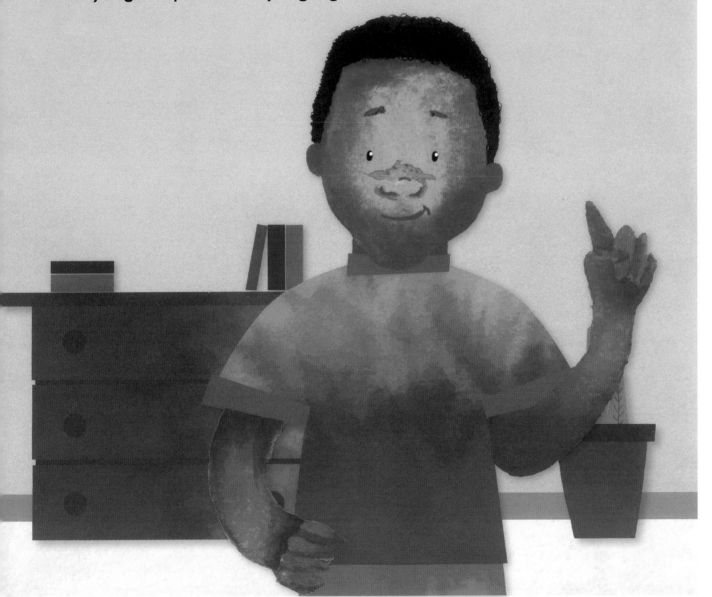

"I'm not sure yet," Riley sighed,
"Cousin Joe, can you help me decide?"
Joe replied, "Of course I can!
Let's give this some thought now, little man."

A moment later, cousin Joe said:
"You could be a chef like Uncle Ted!
Your restaurant could serve breakfast, lunch and dinner,
If you did that, you'd be onto a winner!"

"A chef," said Riley. "That sounds good!
But do you really think I could?"
Joe said: "Your food could be fit for a king.
*Riley, you can be anything!*"

Riley was pleased, but still unsure.
"Maybe we should think some more.
What else could I be?" Riley asked Joe,
"Hmmm," said Joe. "Oh, I know..."

"You could play the saxophone like Uncle Baz,
He's in a band that plays music called jazz.
It's really cool music that's for everyone,
It's funky and groovy and lots of fun."

"I like the saxophone!" Riley cried.
"Are you sure I could play it? I've never tried."
"Of course," said Joe. "You've got that swing.
*Riley, you can be anything!*"

Riley liked the saxophone idea,
But still, there was more he wanted to hear.
He asked cousin Joe: "What else could I be?"
Joe smiled and said: "Hmmm, let's see..."

"I've got it," said Joe. "This is a good plan:
You could be a doctor like Uncle Dan.
When people are ill, you'll make them feel better.
Or you can write them a doctor's letter."

"Make people better?" Riley asked.
"Yes," said Joe. "It's a special task.
Think of all the joy you could bring,
*Riley, you can be anything!*"

Riley was happy – but still he pondered.
"What else could I be?" he sat and wondered.
"Cousin Joe, I'm still not sure."
"No problem," said Joe. "We can think some more."

"But let me have a sip of my drink,
Water always helps me think.
Oh, I know," Joe said as he drank.
"You could be a pilot like Great Grandad Frank!"

"He flew a plane in the Royal Air Force,
That was years ago, of course!
He was brave as he flew in the sky,
Soaring his plane through the clouds way up high."

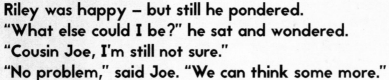

Riley thought for a little while,
And then he gave a massive smile.
"A pilot," he said. "Now that sounds great!
I'm so excited, I can't wait!"

"But up in the clouds is very high,
What if I'm scared to go up in the sky?
Joe smiled and said: "Stop worrying!
*Riley, you can be anything!"*

The next day, Riley was at school,
He was feeling pretty cool.
The things that cousin Joe had said,
Were still whizzing round in Riley's head!

Then the teacher, Mr Brew
Said, "Class, here's what we're going to do:
I'd like you to think and then tell me,
When you grow up, what would you like to be?"

"A teacher," said Lucy, "A fireman," said Kyle.
"I'm going to be a writer," Jane said with a smile.
"A vet," said Eddie, "A dentist," said Bea.
Everyone knew what they wanted to be!

"How about you, Riley?" Mr Brew said,
"I'm not sure yet," said Riley, scratching his head.
But just as the school bell started to ring,
*Riley said... "I can be anything!"*

# RILEY CAN BE ANYTHING

Words by Davina Hamilton
Illustration by Elena Reinoso

**Also from Davina Hamilton:**

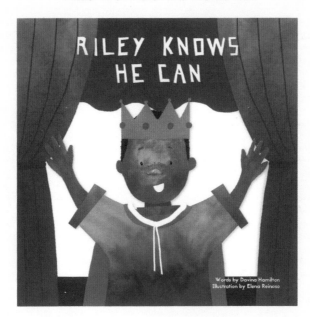

www.davinahamilton.com